seriously SILLY colour

Laurence Anholt · Arthur Robins

Duck!

The Ugly Duck Thing

ORCHARD BOOK

D0272916

In a wooden shack lived
a Mummy Duck.

Mummy Duck laid six brown eggs.

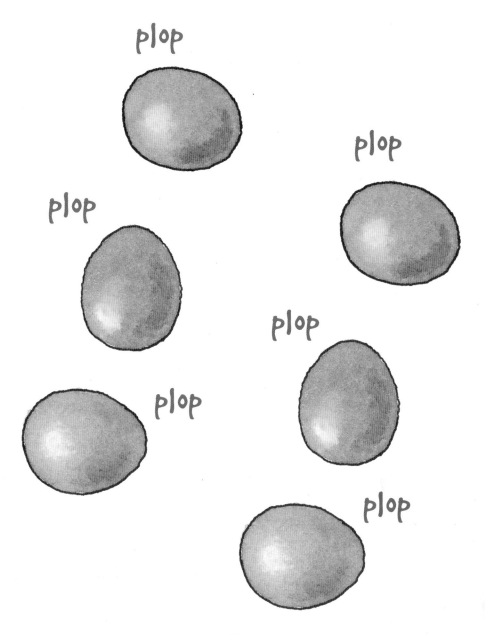

plop

plop

plop

plop

plop

plop

She was very proud.

But one morning,
a bee flew into
the shack.

Quack, quack!
I'm under
attack!

And one lovely egg rolled
off the stack and out of
the back of the shack.

7

At last, Mummy Duck's egg
tumbled into a huge cave.

Quack, quack!
Everything's black!

Mummy Duck fumbled in the dark
and found an egg.

She put the
egg carefully
in her nest
and sat down
to wait.

Then she heard
a little noise.

Quack, quack!
They're starting
to crack!

Crack!

Crack!

Crack!

Crack!

Crack!

Out popped five
tiny, fluffy ducklings.

The little ducklings grew
a tiny bit every day.
But the Ugly Duck Thing
grew huge and HUNGRY!

The Ugly Duck Thing did not
want a tiny worm for tea, he
wanted something much bigger.

18

Mummy Duck taught the five ducklings to swim.

Quack, quack!
You'll soon
get the knack

The Ugly Duck Thing grew
too big to live in the shack.
He decided to go into the world.

He walked a long way. Wherever he went people laughed at him.

Look at that Ugly Duck Thing

The Ugly Duck Thing felt very sad

But the Ugly Duck Thing ate too many trees and lost his job.

The Ugly Duck Thing walked some more and got very lost.

He came to a dark wood
and found a nice cave.

In the cave was . . .

. . . a whole family of big Ugly Duck Things! They were just like him. The Ugly Duck Thing was very happy.

In the corner of the cave was one tiny Duck Thing.

He won't eat anything except worms. He never seems to grow

The Ugly Duck Thing looked at the tiny Duck Thing.

I think I know where you belong

He carried him on his back up the track to the shack.

Mummy Duck was very pleased
to see the Ugly Duck Thing.
And she was even more pleased
to see her own baby duckling.

The Ugly Duck Thing went to live
with his real family in the cave.

They said he was the most beautiful Duck Thing they had ever seen and made him their king.

Enjoy all these
Seriously Silly stories!

Bleeping Beauty	ISBN 978 1 84616 073 8
The Elves and the Storymaker	ISBN 978 1 84616 074 5
The Silly Willy Billy Goats	ISBN 978 1 84616 075 2
The Ugly Duck Thing	ISBN 978 1 84616 076 9
Freddy Frog Face	ISBN 978 1 84616 077 6
Handsome and Gruesome	ISBN 978 1 84616 078 3
The Little Marzipan Man	ISBN 978 1 84616 079 0
The Princess and the Tree	ISBN 978 1 84616 080 6

All priced at £8.99

Orchard books are available from all good bookshops, or can be ordered direct from the publisher:
Orchard Books, PO BOX 29, Douglas IM99 1BQ
Credit card orders please telephone: 01624 836000 or fax: 01624 837033
or visit our website: www.orchardbooks.co.uk or e-mail: bookshop@enterprise.net for details.

To order please quote title, author and ISBN and your full name and address.
Cheques and postal orders should be made payable to 'Bookpost plc.'
Postage and packing is FREE within the UK (overseas customers should add £1.00 per book).

Prices and availability are subject to change.